Buying this book or downloading it you donate 50 cents to the IHP association for the health and the safety of all the mistreated horses:

http://www.horseprotection.it

On their side

Humans don't always learn easily what respect for life is. They don't consider other animals as companions with which to cohabit, but like things to use and throw away afterwards. Horses, more than other species, suffer from this culture, which has little that is natural and a lot that is anthropocentric. A horse is hardly considered a friend, because he is always a horse “to do something”: trotting horse, racing horse, jumping horse, dressage horse, riding school horse, carriage horse, circus horse…slaughtering horse: the same terminology underlines that he doesn't exist as an individual in the average consideration, but only on his utility. He doesn't have rights. IHP was born to encourage a change and to shake consciences: it is our solemn commitment to equines, who make us better persons with their gentleness, their depth and their pride.

THANKS!

SAMANTA CATASTINI

A GUEST AT VERSAILLES

TRANSLATED BY CRISTINA CONTILLI

The heart has its time, you must know how to listen it! (Samanta)

I dedicate this book to Cristina Contilli, my friend and my second soul!

www.italianromances.wordpress.com

I take thee at thy word:
Call me but love, and I'll be new baptis'd;
Henceforth I never will be Romeo.

W.Shakespeare

VERSAILLES CHATEAUX

Versailles, 1769

"I'll never fall in love with any other man." Sophie only had eyes for him, the Count Charles Mercier. Tall, blonde, green eyes and very reserved. Every time she met him, she did everything to exchange a few words with him. He seemed happy to listen her and to be in her company but nothing more. He never suggested an interest in her. Often they strolled together in the gardens of Versailles in silence or talking about horses, a passion shared by both. When she returned to her apartment, with a trembling heart, she threw herself on her

canopy bed and she was dreaming. She had known him five years ago and since then she hoped one day to become his wife. Now, looking in the mirror, wondering what she missed by not awaken her passion. Tall, slightly sallow complexion, brown eyes and long dark red hair. Sixth day of May, a few days earlier, she made twenty-five years old. So already in age to find a husband worthy of her noble title.

Baroness Sophie Lemar, descendant of an ancient French family, was residing at court since her childhood. Then her parents retired in northern France, the enchanting Picardie, in one of their many homes, to monitor more closely their assets land. She had decided to stay in Versailles with her dear friend, the Baroness Camille Noël.

"But why not look elsewhere? There are so many young noblemen who try to get you the court. You can't throw away your youth behind that count. As attractive if she had wanted to ask her in marriage would have already done. "

Sophie looked baffled Camille, sitting beside her bed, without answering. She could not accept the reality, even before the evidence of the facts.

"Yes... But not yet engaged with no lady of the court. Maybe it's just shy and does not find the courage to declare." Camille sighed and then take a serious expression.

"I hope you're right." She risen from her chair in blue velvet and she was spun around.

"Okay, I give up, I don't insist more on this story but only if you swear to me to be more polite and helpful to the guys who try to make your acquaintance. You're always so grumpy away from anyone!"

In recent time, infact, she behaved like a sour old maid. She smiled and she enjoyed only if she was in the same room of Count Mercier, even though he was talking to other people and not paying attention to her. His presence alone put her in a good mood. Perhaps it was time to change strategy. Or better to find one, since there had never thought of before.

"I have just delivered a suit. Do you want me show it?" Camille regained with her usual reassuring smile.

"Come on, let me see what color you chose." Sophie called the waitress who in within five minutes returned with a pretty dress in green silk. The neckline and the sleeves were adorned with yellow lace and the skirt embellished by the classic basket. She looked at the big mirror wall holding him in front of him.

"What do you think? If I add a little of classical feminine malice may become ill some noble heart."
"You are magnificent. I think that few people can resist!"
"Don't overdo it!"
"We'll see tomorrow night at the ball of the king. By the way I heard that there will be a close friend of Louis XV. Count Roland Chevalier, known throughout France for his reputation as a libertine. It seems that all women fall at his feet. Will be a guest at court for a month."
In her mind brought a mischievous idea. So as not wanting to share with mischievous friend. Why not be wooed by this known heartbreaker for jealous Count Mercier? If you really felt something for her he would come the time to take the long-awaited decision.

The Count Roland ecstatically admired the great gardens of Versailles, so immense as not to see the end. The palace seemed so grand and impressive strike from almost afraid. Often, during the festivities in which he took part, he had heard of this architecture flattered across Europe, but he could not imagine that. Now that was traveling in a carriage major avenues could not find a suitable adjective to sum up the beauty. Dared not think that would have reserved the apartment of Louis XV. Half an hour later, with the help of three valets, he reached his rooms. In addition to a very spacious room, complete with canopy bed, he had a bath full of scented oils and linen embroidered. The adjoining sitting room was very comfortable, there were several chairs and a comfortable sofa filled with cushions.

"Monsieur Chevalier soon the king will be on you. Would you like something while you wait?" The young waitress just looked at him, infact, she was so shy.

"Yes, thanks. Bring the Champagne." Though he was accustomed to the pomp, he had to admit that the luxury of this home was beyond any excess. Was curious to find out what it was like the dance that evening. They would miss the pretty girls to woo and many new nobles referred to knowledge.

"At last we meet again." Intention to observe the park from the large windows he didn't notice the entrance, almost silent, the King. Were warmly embraced and then sit facing each other.

"This place is really beautiful!"

"I'm happy that you like. Do you have a good trip?"

"Yes long, but comfortable. The king had taken a cake from a tray of silver lying on the table.
"How's your father? For many years that I didn't see him. I would have liked to receive at court with you."
"He had to resolve administrative problems that otherwise would have come very willingly. He remembers him with great affection." The count Dominic Chevalier had known Louis XV during a hunting trip in northern France. He had felt so much sympathy for this man, fond of good living and beautiful women, to be hosted in his castle for a few days. Picardy had helped the king's health and he promised to return. Then the commitments had become so tight as not to find more time to do so. Roland was still small when he had last seen yet the familiarity that was initiated at that time still seemed intact.
"Tonight you will have opportunity to meet many beautiful ladies, already aware of your reputation as a libertine before even having seen."
"With this reputation I will flee as soon as I will see all." The king smiled and gave him a pat on the shoulder.
"Women are tremendously attracted to scoundrels and... even to the titles!

The Hall of Mirrors was beautifully lit and so crowded that she could not discern even the royal family. Sophie walked beside Camille sure that since he left his apartment, talked incessantly. She wore the green dress that she had just bought and she dressed her hair with the flowers. The friend, however, chose a white dress adorned with lace heaven. They looked like twin sisters for their identical hair color and eyes but also for their close harmony. As a child, they had shared the joys and sorrows, the games and studies, so as to become inseparable. Precisely because both only children knew they could rely on each other.

"Look there's the Count Mercier" Sophie started to turn from side to side without seeing the crowd.

"Calm down and stop! He was in the back along with the Baron and Baroness Dubois. Please do not go straight to him. Keep a bit away to see how he reacts. You are always in front to his feet." Camille could not give her best advice. The buzz of voices drowned the background music. In the jubilant crowd had seen a handful of women around a tall man with hair shiny blacks, like the thousands of lighted candles through the tunnel, eyes blacks and a winning smile. She had been very

slow in understanding that must be the famous Count Roland Chevalier and, given his undeniable beauty, she was not surprised because he had so many women around. At that moment she realized that he had attracted his attention because it was detached from the fray and, with quick steps and elegant, it was directed towards her and Camille.

"Sophie, what must be the Count Chevalier, the host of the king. Oh, God, he is coming to us." A whirlwind of emotions and thoughts crowded her mind as the gentleman dressed in green had bowed. Then, his firm handshake had passed a warmth that she never felt before. Looks bold man had put her in a little uncomfortable, but she tried not to show it. Her pride was always able to win in every situation.

"Good evening, I am the Count Roland Chevalier with whom I have the honor of speaking?"

"I am the Baroness Sophie Lemarié and this is my dear friend, the Baroness Camille Noël. A furtive glance had settled on both but he had lingered longer on her. She had been wrong to think at this famous libertine for jealous Count Mercier. Now she had to run the show...

Although he had before him many beautiful ladies, young and available, his eyes were resting on the girl looking rebellious and appealing at the same time. She had a strange hair color and complexion amber that stood out in the midst of all the other perfectly white, even with the use of a lot of powder. Gave off a fresh scent of lavender that had enveloped him when she looked him with the typical arrogance of a woman sure of herself. He quickly realized that she did not receive any adulation or even less, any indecent proposal. Maybe that was her coldness to attract. She was indifferent to his bewitching eyes, indeed she seemed almost angry. In admiration to her chaste dress he had felt the urge to hug her and to kiss her before all the courtiers. A smile had the idea that deep just imagine the uproar that would come.

"I'd like explained under the beautiful gardens of the palace? Take a leisurely stroll, of course accompanied by your girlfriend and my butler Damien?" Sophie had turned to seek solace by her friend as she suffered in a reassuring smile.

"Okay I accept your invitation. But just because you are a guest of our beloved sovereign, and as such I hope that you behave politely towards two women just met!" Her reaction was to be angry instead tried to understand it. His reputation

as a libertine preceded him in court was therefore obvious that a good and serious girl felt in trouble in his presence.

"I could never dishonor two friends of the king of France. I am aware that you have heard bad opinions about me but please check volervene alone, I promise you I will not do anything to make you feel in danger." The group of noblewomen, who shortly before had surrounded, had approached stealthily.

"Count Chevalier, do you accompany us to drink a glass of Champagne, while you tell us of your estates?" The Marquise Dufour launched a challenge to Sophie's eyes remained impassive.

"I'm sorry but the count was with Mademoiselle through the gardens. I can always reach you later, isn't true?" Roland looked her surprised and he had stretched out his hand.

"Yes and I will make you notice my presence just returned from our walk. Please, do you excuse us?" The noble women were reluctant to open mouth, while a little farther on, a gentleman with an imposing physique and blond watched them leave...

She still could not understand how she had immediately accepted the curious proposal of the Count. The effrontery of the Marquise Dufour had exceedingly annoyed that pushed almost into the arms of the attractive stranger. They were walking along the Grand Canal, followed by Camille Butler and the young Damien, in complete silence. Every now and then, with the corner of my eye, tried to examine it without being seen. He was well formed cheekbones, dark eyes gaze deep and a high forehead and large, who bear a tuft of hair rebellious blacks. His physique, powerful and muscular, remembered the ancient Greek statues depicting the gods of Olympus. She blushed suddenly remembering that they were naked men.

"Do you feel hot?" Although there were many candles lit around the garden side the Grand Canal, she hoped that he had not noticed the sudden, her color instead...

"No, absolutely! Indeed. The air is very fresh and pleasant."

"So you're thinking of something forbidden or shameful because your pretty cheeks are suddenly flushed."

"How dare you think such a thing? Believe that every woman is hopelessly attracted to you? You are very presumptuous!" Laughter was even more nervous that Sophie looked at him scornfully.

"You are very beautiful when you get angry!" As far as intimacy and friendship there had always been between her and the Count Mercier she had never been asked such a compliment. Or rather she never received appreciation or for her appearance or for what they wore. The chatter behind them had them spun around and had allowed each of them to forget what happened.

"Really? You are so cute!" Camille was laughing so next to Damien that was holding his right arm. Astonished by his nearness, among other things not suited to two people of very different rank, Sophie had stopped shooting awaiting their arrival.

"Ah, Count Chevalier, is so pleasant company of your butler." The young boy had lowered his eyes as a sign of discomfort, in front of his master. He was tall and dark hair, eyes, curious and lively, with deep blue color.

"I know! Without her love of life bore me to death!" Camille took him back to the arm and had reached a bench stone.

"Tell me count fair wind brought you to Versailles after the conquest of other noblewomen?"

"My reputation as a libertine, there has just hit. Do you could not get to the head?"

"It's not easy when a handful of women throw themselves at you like hounds on their prey!"
"Maybe you women much more interested in a man to marry to avoid that one!" had to admit that was a witty and opinionated person. If he wanted to make him a worthy suitor could not attack her but continually try to show curious to know everything about her life.
"Perhaps! But as you already got to understand I'm not that kind of woman. I like the tranquility and complete honesty." He had accepted the hand he was holding out to help her sit on the edge of a fountain, trying to sound at ease.
"Then I will be honest as possible with you. I came to court because as my father entertain a nice match with the king had never had occasion either to know Versailles or Paris. I love living in the north of France, but it was time to admire the magnificence real. I also need a little rest. You think that I spend all my time behind the skirts of every lady I meet, however, I have better things to do in my castle. I take care of production and marketing of our wine... I hope you want to taste a glass because I did send a lot of bottles to our beloved sovereign."

Sophie listened carefully and then she looked around to make sure that Camille and Damien were always nearby.

"In any case, if your reputation has preceded you rake it must be a reason. Like the fact that you are not yet married, after all belong to an ancient and very wealthy family, the dream of every girl."

"I have just said! In the past I have had many stories, especially with married women or widows, tired of their husbands in search of excitement. Let me close with this part of my life and be able to find a nice lady to share my future." In uttering that last sentence had become serious and thoughtful.

"It will be very easy to delete an opinion so entrenched in society. You know that some definitions may accompany us throughout life."

"Why do not you help me?" Sophie stared at him shocked and could hardly answer.

"I can help you? And how?"

"Could you give me some tips on how to converse with girls respectable. Unfortunately I doubt that a respectable young woman want to marry me. Attract only women who want to have fun for a night and then..." She blushed at the very idea of such meetings enthusiasts. Yet something inside her she told

to Sophie that she had to give him a hope. She warned in his words a social isolation that made him suffer.
"Although not the most qualified will be happy to help in that!"

When he was returned to his room, he had thrown himself exhausted on the bed. Damien had helped him to undress and then he withdrew to his room. He seemed to feel even the fresh scent of Sophie. That girl was not only beautiful, but also very intelligent. She had listened politely and never stop and never taking his eyes if not to find her friend, the Baroness Camille. Tired of his amorous adventures without emotional commitment, he felt a jolt to the heart every time he spoke. His amber skin and gave her an exotic appearance, in his opinion, even more fine other noblewomen known at Versailles. For the first time in his life, thirty years of age, she was kidnapped from his presence and was left confused. He never makes love could not tell if that was the feeling as sung by poets. In any case, his desire to see her was so strong that he can hope to arrive before the following morning. They had not given a precise date, but he would discover her in some corner of this vast golden palace. Damien Or perhaps, given his obvious sympathy for Camille, it would be helpful. Decides to ring the bell to summon in the room.

"Tell me, Roland, are you looking for me?"

"Yes! For now you have been very good but you try not to call me before others I should pretend otherwise punish you and you know I'm not very good at acting! "

"I'm sorry but it is not easy to succeed in maintaining that part... but at least I managed to see Versailles!" He sat on the chair near the bed and he had a long sigh.

"Listen, dear Baroness Noël, did you informed about her habits and those of Mademoiselle Sophie?"

"You are looking for new emotions?"

"Don't make jokes! This time, I wish to behave like a true knight, but I don't know how to go in the right place in the right time!"

"I know that every morning is a long ride in the royal gardens." Roland stood up out of bed and he was aimed at the large window that faces onto the Grand Canal.

"Good. Then I will go to inform the stables to rent two horses... Oh I forgot, I don't make jokes to Baroness Camille or I will ruin my arduous conquest."

"And who wants to make fun of her? I have just two words to decide that this will be the mother of my children. Whatever the cost!"

She had woken up very early to arrive not later at the rendezvous with the Count Mercier. As they rode together in the park every morning and then, after a leisurely breakfast, they return to their apartments. Sophie always wait anxiously for sharing those moments with the man who wanted more than anything else in the world. If her plan had succeeded and the count was jealous she might realize her dream. She tried not to fantasize over this goal area for years and had thrown off the bed. After wearing a comfortable dress, pink soft, cotton and without a basket, to be able to ride better, had rushed to the stables.

"Hello Mademoiselle Lemaire, the Count is waiting for you already on horseback." Pierre, the young groom, had hastened to saddle Noir, his great black stallion. He had helped her to rise. When he reached Charles, she had noticed once that I was in high spirits as each morning.

"May I have been delayed?

"No, I'm just not able to sleep well and I got up earlier than usual. How are you?" As soon as he had turned his smile she always felt melt like snow in the sun.

"Very good and you?"

"Good! I would only make you a little note before beginning our ride." In uttering those words had made her look stern and gloomy. Sophie had felt a pang as when a child waiting for a rebuke from his father.

"Tell me well."

"I think it is very unwise for you to spend time with that damn rake, the Count Chevalier. Is not worthy of a pure and noble woman brought up like you!" For a split second she felt the thrill of victory. The choice to accept his courtship had had the desired effect. For once Charles had noticed her in the middle of a royal reception. In all those years had never happened. Usually, when they were around people, he just say hello and then continued on his way.

"So why not try to protect and to abide more closely?" The Count Mercier had started at a gallop without answering. Sophie had followed him in silence. Only after half an hour he stopped and gave a hand to help her down. The sun began peeking through the clouds in the morning while the songs of

birds delight the country feel. They were sitting on the grass to admire the fresh immense palace that loomed in the distance almost like a mirage.

"I don't think that you need my help or my presence to expel this impostor. You must be to discourage him." Damn, that was not exactly the answer that she hoped to receive. She had to make another attempt before thinking that the plan had failed.

"You just said I'm an educated person and therefore do not think is nice to contact or with pride or arrogance of a man who looks kindly. It is not my intention. For this I ask you a little support. If only we could present ourselves as closely as possible, perhaps could be moved." For fear of a refusal to this proposal she began to play her right nervously with the folds of her skirt. Had spent a minute that seemed an eternity. Then Charles turned and he smiled softly, breaking the ice curtain that enveloped him regularly.

"Okay. I'll be by your side in the name of friendship that binds us for many years." It was not exactly the phrase that she wanted to hear, but it was enough to hope for something more.

"Hello, Count Mercier and honored to see you again Baroness Lemarié." On a horse dappled brown and white the famous

libertine, monsieur Chevalier, was smiling like a king who has just won a coveted city.

The look with which the young Sophie was addressing the Count Mercier showed no friendship, but a kind of adoration. It was as if, at that time, there existed no other person in the world. She could not take your eyes off him. He had the impression that he had broken something with his sudden arrival.

"What do you bring, Monsieur Chevalier? You are already hunting for new conquests?" The tone was contemptuous of the count and even provocative.

"Why should do it, I when I see before my eyes one of the most beautiful women who I've ever seen in my life?" Sophie blushed and she lowered her eyes, pretending to look for something in the grass.

"Mademoiselle Lemaire is a respectable person so as not to need your courtship. There are many gentlemen who are only waiting for a sign from her to come forward. I advise you to look for entertainment elsewhere." The contemptuous tone of

this man had irritated but did not want to fall into his trap. So he always flaunted a radiant smile and a kindness almost unnatural. It would be easier to respond in kind but he had the desired effect.

"I don't try any pastime, but only to know a gentle and respectable person. Not all the women I meet have to end up in my bed!" Sophie burst into laughter, perhaps to defuse the bad air that was pulling between the two.

"The Count Chevalier was really second to none! Why not accompanied me to the stables?" Charles had turned a startled look.

"Don't worry about me, Monsieur Mercier. I'm sure that in broad daylight our dear libertine will hold off his innermost instincts!"

She must insist now that Charles seemed annoyed by the clear advances of the Count Chevalier. He could have just played the part of man jealous. Or at least, it was which Sophie had hoped. Within minutes they had reached the stables. Roland rode quickly and turned often to make sure of his presence. The groom Pierre had helped her to fall and before bringing the horse in his box with the count looked puzzled.

"Did you have changed your knight on the way?" The young boy spoke the word as an equal with the confidence of friendship that she had shown since their first meeting.

"Yes I met Monsieur Chevalier during rest and he has offered to accompany me." The went up almost a whisper he told her: "So much the better! If you really do I have to say that Count Mercier I do not like at all. He is so sophisticated. Always serious and steady. He isn't the man for you!" Sophie smiled but she had been unable to answer.

"Sorry if I intruded into your privacy, but since many years I wanted to tell you. You are so sunny and happy who have lost their desire to live next to someone so gloomy. Suddenly he had bowed and was gone. Mademoiselle, do you want to follow me?" Roland was holding out his arm, smiling and protective as the night before.

"Sure, where will you take me?"

"Don't worry. Not in my apartments."

"You never fail to repeat that. If I have to teach you how you should speak to a lady is my duty to emphasize that this is a misstep. Able only to embarrass the girl that you have before you the result of her immediate rejection."

"So I asked you to help me. But, I must admit that your beauty distracts me and I delight at the same time."

"To be a good student you have to remove those thoughts from your mind otherwise you will remain with your bad name!" She was journeying to the square of access to the palace where a coach is waiting for them. As soon as the coachman opened the door Camille was down in a hurry to embrace her friend.

"Hello Sophie. How nice to see you in the early morning."

"But... I don't understand..." Roland helped her to rise. Inside, the butler Damien had smiled and he made space for her on comfortable red velvet chair.

"My dear, I wanted to take you on a delightful walk in the garden of Saint Cloud. The Duke of Orleans gave me permission to visit and I didn't want to deprive you of such a pleasure!" The pleasant surprise of the girl had filled him with pride and hope. At least for a few hours would be able to eclipse in his heart the picture of his new enemy, Count Mercier.

She always wanted to see the castle of the Duke, but she was never invited to any party. The nobles who came to the delightful walks in the great Italian gardens or the magnificent receptions, they spoke very well. Silently they were watching the road from the window, while Camille and Damien spoke to each other almost in a whisper. Even without turning the count felt his eyes on her. She didn't know if she was happier to finally visit this architectural masterpiece, or the proximity of the man who, despite rumors, he seemed polite and respectful as well as very attractive. He was really nice, his body was so athletic and powerful to attract the attention of both young women who mature.

"Are you happy or you my call I just made a hardship?" His voice seemed really curious to know his opinion on the matter.

"But you're kidding? I have done a really pleasant surprise!" He stood smiling sweetly even though his eyes still lingering on his caste cleavage. Fortunately she had worn a garment very comfortable that had no problem in enjoying the show that the country would be.

"We don't visit the castle, because the Duke is away on business, but has asked me not to indulge in what we want to pry into the park. The butlers will serve us a nice lunch

outdoors. More she looked, the more she convinced her of his incomparable elegance, so well designed that it seems natural. He was wearing a fabulous coat of green with dark brown pants and leather boots knight clear. The shirt, in white silk, was a bit on his chest and then deprived of scarves. At first glance it might seem like a match but then she felt rushed at once, thanks to the precious textiles, almost maniacal accuracy. The fresh scent of sandalwood pleasantly enveloped the cockpit of the car. Soon as they arrived in front of the great barred gate, two guards on either side, after a careful examination of the written invitation of the Duke, had given them permission to enter. The view of the park was so grand and majestic breathtaking. The intent of equal Versailles had driven the Duke in an enterprise but down the magnificent palace. The gardens were so big that they do not see the end. All crowned with large fountains and streams that delighted the ears thanks to the happy songs of birds. Countless statues adorned every corner of the park and the beautiful terrace of the Orangerie in Paris allowed a view of breathtaking.

The Count Chevalier had asked the driver to stop at the Bassin des Cygnes and when they got out of the cab the sound of water gushing stifled all their ecstatic comment. The fountain, designed by Girard between 1672 and 1675, had a huge basin in the shape of a horseshoe. Camille had launched an amused glance at Sophie who had taken the opportunity to take her arm and apartments in his company.

"What are you doing with Damien? Do you seem to be too lenient towards him?"

" You're worrying for nothing." She kept smiling dreamily.

"He was a butler! You realize that arise when the scandal continue to Versailles to see you in his company? You will be disgraced and banned for life from high society."

Before returning from his new suitor she took Sophie's arm forcing her to follow her.

"Damien hides a noble secret. Don't feel sorry for me!"

For Roland seeing her so happy and eager to visit every corner innermost of these magnificent parks made him proud to have her conduct there. Fortunately the weather was sunny and a light breeze cooled the air spring. Yet his thoughts turned increasingly to the expression of Sophie as she listened spellbound the Count Mercier. He could not think about her and he had confidence that proves all the love that look of the young girl towards that cold individual. He was in trouble and he could not have confidence in his renowned skills of libertine.

"Monsieur Chevalier why do we not achieve? What are you doing there all alone?" Camille was calling because deep in his thoughts had not noticed that he was far behind the others. He had reached Sophie, intent to have every single sculpture or fountain, which met during the journey, would stand by his side.

"Can I tell you that today you are really beautiful? Your eyes seem to reflect happiness of your soul!"

"Then why do you keep staring at my décolletage? Do I make you again because a fine gentleman should behave not so. At least this time you have given a nice compliment, but... you have to hold off your look cocky. Roland was unable to suppress a smile.

"Why I try to close otherwise fit as possible! To learn how to behave in a manner appropriate to my right and title of nobility. " She was focused and she smiled back.

"Meanwhile you are able to do a nice compliment that every lady would have appreciated." She approached her mouth to whisper in her ear something.

"In any case your neck, though caste, lets imagine a body invited to be discovered."

"But you are outrageous! Never change!" Her cheeks were flushed with shame and with a rush, had suffered a direct briskly toward the dear friend. For the rest of the journey had not spoken, but something told him this compliment was not in vain. They had reached the terrace of the Orangerie where, after admiring the beautiful panorama of Paris, some butlers were sumptuously prepared a table for four people. The tablecloth, a beautiful white silk, shining in the sunlight as well as dishes of Sevres porcelain and precious silver cutlery engraved with the initials of the Duke of Orleans.

"Please Mademoiselle Lemaire and Mademoiselle Camille do you sit down?" Damien had moved the chairs padded to allow the two noble ladies to sit down. As soon as he had settled at the table they admired the brilliant dishes.

"This is a wonderful dishes encrypted."

"Do you know this famous manufactory count was promoted and supported financially by Madame de Pompadour, the famous mistress of our king. She had a taste and sophistication unrivaled. Only thanks to her we can admire these works of

art." Roland had left to pay a little white wine in the cup while she stood up and look at your plate.

"I've heard very good and yet his fame is free of vile slander that have been addressed." Sophie had a napkin lying on his legs and, with a rush, she was launched in defense of the baroness.

"My mother has always spoken very highly of her, calling it a very generous and infinitely acculturation. Our literature and our art should be grateful. In the short time in which I had the opportunity to meet her I know her sweetness opposed to her strong personality."

"I must say that there is a credit to your intent to elevate to posthumous glory!" The eyes of the girl had grown still more gloomy and nervous.

"Her person does not need any help to me. In the future we will talk a lot about her and the positive opinions far surpass the views negative."

A waiter had served a copious platter of crawfish and a copious salad scented with boiled eggs.

"When something upsets to you, you have a character to sell."

"I know that you have visited the gardens of Saint Cloud. Were to your liking?" The king, Louis XV, was sitting in the middle of his apartment, while a waiter was serving the wine fresh.

"Yes, I would say very nice and well cared for but so lower wing magnificence of those at Versailles." He could not give such a disappointment to the sovereign, after all, the palace and its huge park could not be compared with any other architectural work in France.

"You've already put their eyes on a young lady?" She didn't know if that question was random or if it was a reflection of his already well-known reputation as a libertine.

"Sire, I haven't come to court to make new conquests or to find the woman of my life, but only for the curiosity and the desire to see you." The waiter showed him a tray full of cookies, but Roland had mentioned not liking.

"This thought makes you honor, but you should not lose sight of the joys of women who populate these rooms during the dances and receptions. You'll be sorry." She smiled to the King and had admired the walls, covered with purple cloth, on which stood out the frames glazed in pure gold. The sunlight that came in through the large windows half closed, created a

play of color almost blinding. For a moment he had thought to shut up but then, retracing in his mind the profound friendship of Louis XV with his father, he decided to give him some questions about Sophie.

"Here... I would honestly put my eyes on a young lady, but I was quite shy and overly serious."

"Oh, where did you see? Here in court? Can not be, every woman does everything to be noticed and to be courted."

"Yes, she is the Baroness Lemaire." The king laughed heartily.

"You have chosen the most chaste of the whole court. Her parents have imposed strict upbringing so it looks like a nun. I was very surprised when they chose to leave her alone at Versailles."

"Why did they go?"

"They live in Picardy to monitor their properties. It's strange that you don't know them."

"Maybe... In any case I think it will not be able to reduce her Iron Curtain. She is always very reserved. Louis XV, after having nibbled on the last biscuit, had risen and he had picked up his jacket lying on the big four-poster bed.

"You have no fear, I saw how the women look towards you. Even my dear mistress, Madame du Barry, has laid eyes on

you. If you will bring your patience, she will yield flattery. Make her understand that the person you want most in the world. It always works." A butler helped him to wear the jacket in silk brocade. Before leaving his room he turned toward the count, who had just turned up to greet him.
"I was forgetting it, I will expect you tomorrow in the afternoon for an enjoyable hunt."

"You have acted like a stupid spoiled child. Before you ask me to close otherwise fit and then, without hesitation, you accepted the invitation of the Count Chevalier. Charles was waiting her at the door of her apartment. Serious and indignant he was coming toward her with a furious look.
Camille, just heard the first words, decided to say goodbye to Sophie immediately to remove the noise. The kiss on the cheek had whispered in her ear: "Don't be intimidated." Those few words had to Sophie the courage to give up her chin and to look Charles straight in the eye.
"Count Mercier do you want to sit down to taste a tea with the exquisite pastries?" After an initial delay, he had to be led by the maid in a private lounge. Suffered drank steaming cup just laid on the table. With a gesture he had settled the maniacal

blond tufts left the tape hairdressing admiring pleasure in great gilt mirror on the wall.

"I'm so sorry to justify a rude refusal. I also noticed that you have not much insisted on keeping me with you."

"What was I supposed to do? Throw myself at your feet?" Her hands, like her heart, had begun to tremble. She could not explain for which, despite adoring the incutesse still much fear. While spending time with her was very difficult to decipher his expression cold and often expressionless. It seemed that he wanted to hide behind a mask so as not to let well-studied vent to his innermost feelings.

"There I asked then. I only hoped there'd be pleased to protect me. If I have offended you with my reckless behavior I offer my deepest apology. It will not happen again." She got up and had turned his gaze out into the beautiful park of the palace, but not to support his anger. I felt movement behind her and the only idea, made her feel uncomfortable. Then she felt his hand on his shoulder and, without turning, she was blushing. She felt his breath on her neck.

"Excuse me. I must admit that I was very abrupt with you. Please forgive me for not only accept my deepest apology but also an invitation to dinner tonight."

"I am very honored to meet you Madame du Barry." The young mistress of the king smiled while Roland had knelt to kiss her hand. She had long blonde hair styled in large curls that fell over her shoulders. The eyes were bright blue, made even brighter thanks to the translucent complexion. The nose, very small, was an absolute perfection. At first glance gave the impression of a very frail as he was able to weave intrigues worthy of a queen. The king had wanted to appear in person. I had sent in his private apartments, those open to a few close friends and ignored by the other courtiers.

"Are you happy to have visited the palace? The room that we have assigned to you is your liking?" When he spoke he was posing his beautiful hands and his ringed eyes turned towards the Cradle ruler who seemed to have eyes for her.

"I could claim to feel a king!" The Du Barry had started to unfurl the full range of feathers to cover her mouth while laughing at the joke made by a taste for the count. He knew he was young and so beautiful as to attract every male gaze on her. Smelt fresh and clean as any other woman of the court. Did not wear wigs or boring but I loved to become covered

with gaudy basket jewelry. The king was saved by the apparent depression in which he had fallen after the death of Madame de Pompadour tasting the fresh meat of this woman ready to do anything to live in luxury. When he discovered the dubious origin of the new concubine, he pretended not to believe it. Now since than sixty years with this girl he had returned to live. Never mind that she was a whore top village, the past for Louis XV did not matter as the present. To make her happy he had spared no expense, luxury residences, clothes, shoes, handbags had almost sunk the royal coffers.

"I am very honored to have made your acquaintance, but, if you permit to me, I would like to retire in my apartment to rest. Tomorrow we are facing a long day's ride, I want to enjoy this hunt real." He had no desire to stay with her and he want to switch to healthier Sophie. After carefully knelt to kiss the hand of Du Barry, he traveled almost ran the courtyard of the deer. That woman, however beautiful she was, he had disgusted. As soon as he passed near the apartments of the Count Mercier he had been attracted by the noise that arrive more than a nice classical chamber music. He had approached the door, where two valets perhaps waiting for the guests. He was detained by the desire to peek inside knowing that it was unbecoming to a

gentleman. Yet something made him hesitate and he prevented him from continuing to his rooms. At that moment he had warned of steps behind him and as soon as he turned he found himself face to face with the very beautiful Sophie.

He was there in front of her who was clearly admired for her clothing. On this occasion she chose a simple dress, no basket in ivory silk with a bodice full of pink ribbons and lace. She had tried not to show her embarrassment and she had given him a warm smile.

"What a coincidence count Chevalier that you are here."

"I was coming back into my apartment after spending the afternoon with the king. And you? Where you are going so elegantly dressed?"

"I was invited by Monsieur Mercier at a dinner in his rooms."

She didn't understand for wich reason, but that appointment was announced almost with shame. It had seemed that the count had not appreciated this news. She must recognize that he was really attractive, with his bright red dress in contrast with his bright hair blacks. Anything he wore made him unparalleled elegance. The noises coming from the living room of Charles had reported sharply to reality. She had to enter as soon as possible if he had seen in the company of the Count would go on a rampage. And she did not like it when he held a grudge. She would have been able to do an embarrassing rebuke before valets and waiters present. When he got angry he could not have brakes. It was not easy to believe that a man looked so angelic might lose his temper so easily.

"I'm sorrym, but I have to go I don't think that it was polite to made them wait."

Roland bowed and he kissed her right hand. In times to enter the apartments of M. Mercier had felt a shiver along the spine. He knew that was not the thrill of crossing the door, but he didn't want to get more questions about what could have her disturbed. Before the attendants told her the way forward to reach the living room had launched a last look at the count. Shoulders seemed even higher. With the lights of many candles her person was projected over the entire length of the corridor.

"Good evening, Mademoiselle Lemaire. But as you are smart."

The voice of a woman made her wince. Baroness Coraline Dubois was comfortably sitting on the chaise in blue satin while the husband was talking with Count Mercier. In this vision Sophie had realized how foolish she had been in waiting for a romantic dinner.

"What a pleasure to see you madame. It will be an honor to spend some hours in your company." She finished the sentence with such a disgust to hope that his faint smile had hidden his disappointment. The baroness was a striking beauty. Blonde, green eyes and very fair. It was said that he had married Monsieur Dubois, twenty years older, just to acquire a social position. Rumors about his past dubious. She had many stories, despite his young age, especially with noble already married. Only by Madame du Barry, his dear childhood friend, had met the baron and was able to get married despite the bad rumors about her reputation. She liked to dress eccentrically and adored the generous necklines that highlight her breasts prosperous.

"Come here and sit Mademoiselle Sophie." Charles was holding out his hand to help her sit. He was limited to her a bow and a polite smile. The Baron Dubois received them much more warmly. The table was set with a beautiful tablecloth, pink and white porcelain dishes. The center were placed two huge silver candlesticks. Throughout the dinner, meat and delicious chicken consommé with vegetables, the Baroness talked incessantly. Mainly clothes and accessories, her favorite topics. Sophie, not to offend her, she feigned interest, but she

was bored to death. Charles and the Baron delighted in political speeches and financial. The thing which was most sad for her it was that he had never sent a single glance from the beginning of dinner. When arrived the dessert, she had not felt obliged to continue the recitation and the banal excuse of a severe headache she was greeted warmly and she retired herself to her room.

When he was back in their apartments, he found Damien and Camilla were having dinner in the lounge. "Roland sorry but I didn't know that you would come back from the appointment with the king or I would have expected." Astonished by the familiarity with which the friend had addressed him, he didn't responde immediately, but he given him a look of reproach. Damien had immediately understood what he meant.

"Don't worry Camille knows everything about me. I could not lie." Then Roland had thrown the chair beside the fireplace in marble and had loose hair. She tried not to look at the girl because of its resemblance to her friend was really embarrassing.

"What were you eating?"

"An exquisite seafood dressed with mayonnaise and hard boiled eggs. Join us will definitely hungry." He took off the bulky coat and was sitting between the two. A waiter had once served the dish and spilled white wine very cold.

"But this is my wine!"

"I don't want if I did open a bottle to try to Mademoiselle Noël. The girl, she felt pulled in the ball, had given him an affectionate smile.

"It's really delicious! Should I give my most sincere congratulations." At first bite, he realized that you have really hungry. I thought they had to leave so busy in the background the basic needs. If he touched the bed at that moment would have sunk into a deep sleep. Damien was explaining the art of wine to Baroness Camille, who seemed attentive and amused by the unusual subject. Given the intimacy and familiarity with the young lady had plucked up courage and he decided to askto her some questions about her dear friend.

"You know very well that Mademoiselle Sophie could you tell me if there is granted, if he has an affair with Count Mercier?" He was almost regretting sincerity of the request made but he needed to know.

"To be honest, and I want to be with you, she is very infatuated. Yet they are years that they spend much time together but he still did not intend to do any kind of proposal." Seemed in trouble but gave the impression of wanting to continue. He was lying on towel near the plate and, after shaking the hand of Damien, had made a big sigh before continuing.
"It isn't the man for her. For months that I continue to repeat this litany, but is more stubborn than a mule. His coldness and arrogance can not marry the joy and simplicity of Sophie. I think that she will never demand that you expect for years. Otherwise you would have already done."
Roland drank another glass of wine then stood up and threw his napkin on the table. He sat on the chair in front of the red satin large window overlooking the Grand Canal.
"What could I do for change her mind?" Camille had reached was sitting at his side. When they first came face to face she had smiled then, looking at the landscape outside had given the advice that he hoped so.
"Be gentle, but don't suffocate her. With timeshe she will know who really loves her!"

They ridden in perfect silence for over an hour later they had stopped in front of the Fontaine de Laton. Sophie had initially liked the sound of water gushing occupying harmoniously those silent moments later she could not suppress his desire to speak.

"Tonight you will come to attend the concert in the grove of the Salle de Bal?" Charles was watching the fountain and the air seemed to have absorbed in other thoughts.

"I do n't think so. Let me rest for a moment. It isn't easy to take part in all events that are celebrated at Versailles." Since she had known him, he had never missed one. Lately he had given the impression of wanting to hide something. Had never been a great orator, but in recent months he had shown less inclination to talk than usual. The only topic that maybe it would make him say was the outcome of the dinner the night before.

"Do you have entertained until late yesterday?"

"Not much. We talked a little and then he met Madame du Barry." The name of the royal mistress made her wince. Could not imagine the Count Mercier in his company. Although endowed with a beauty out of the ordinary was a woman of

dubious origins and was expressed in a language not quite a lady.

"How strange that our sovereign charm is made by a person other than Madame de Pompadour." At these words, Charles had spun around and his big green eyes had seemed to see a bit of anger.

"What do you mean? Madame is a very intelligent woman and love of Louis XV. It amazes me that a lady as you listen to these silly rumors of court." Sophie looked at him with amazement and almost with fear. She had never seen so taken in defending the integrity of a friend. When the count Chevalier had openly courted did not even bother to go to his aid. He was she, under his explicit request, to push him to do so. Now, after this his impulsive reaction, was no longer sure they want his support. Especially because it was not sincere but rather a choice set. Anyway that morning had shown that when a person was really at the heart was able to defend and could do so with enthusiasm emotional.

"You are right that I should not speak. I don't know so well her as Madame Dubois. I know that their friendship goes back to childhood days. He was lying on the grass and closed his eyes.

"We have studied in the same convent and we have always remained in contact. Then fate would have it, they met again here in the court." The night before she had noticed how many times the baroness had exchanged glances with his languid, Count Mercier. She had not wanted to jump to conclusions about her, but now after listening to his words began to have doubts. His fervor in defending was really impressive and, sincerante, unjustified. Furthermore, how could he be so well informed about the early life of Madame Dubois?

"Congratulations Monsieur Chevalier you're really a good hunter. I hope you will take me again at other bars in the coming days." The king was dismounting from his horse helped by his attendants and the other nobles were already reaching their apartments. Despite his advanced age, the king was always a very athletic man. They had ridden for more than two hours without stopping.

"For me it will be an honor to take part in another hunt." Madame du Barry had immediately approached Louis XV and she had left her kiss on the cheeks. Then she turned a languid glance at Roland who, ignoring, in a few moments had reached

the exit of the stables. Was tempted to go to visit to Sophie, but he knew that he would see her the same evening during the concert in the grove of the Salle de Bal. Arrived in his apartment he found a note where Damien said that he had decided to take a walk in the park with Camille. He had just fallen asleep immediately touched the bed. When he opened his eyes off it was already dark. In a panic he had looked at the clock on the wall. Nine. Within half an hour would begin the concert. In time to take a hot tub and dressing in a hurry.

"I hesitated to wake you. How are you? Did you spend a nice afternoon with the king?" Damien, standing in the doorway of the room, watching him, amused. Since he met Camille was always smiling and cheerful.

"You had better jump off the bed. So I can be late for the concert! "

A footman stood holding out a large towel encrypted while another was taken to the bathroom a big tub full of boiling water.

"Do not be worthwhile Sophie and Camille have yet to prepare! We returned an hour ago from a long walk in the park. "

"What was he doing with you, Sophie?" Roland was soaking in the tub, while her friend was sitting in the chair beside busy and do some scented oils for the toilets.

"It was a bit down for the count's fault and Camille Mercier insisted to bring with us. My dear I think that now is your moment of opportunity ". He emerged from the water with his head and looked at him quizzically.

"What do you mean?" The dull thud of glass on the floor, announcing the breaking of a jar of lavender-scented oil. Footman was immediately rushed to clean up the precious white marble.

"Oh God forgive me are still the same careless!"

"It's not news! So you tell me what you talk about?"

"It was very sad because it seems no Mercier Monsieur them the proposal that a long wait. Also this morning seems to be stubborn in defending Madame du Barry. Sophie I was upset and if I can afford, I think its an insult to a woman so serious as you. The concubine of the king seems to be a great friend of Baroness Coraline Dubois, assiduous frequenters of all parties is the court that the Opera. It is rumored that it is precisely her passion for the power to have led her to marry a man much older than her. The rest preferred to remain silent because her

past does not differ much from real favorite. Her husband is a close acquaintance of the count and perhaps also share some economic interest." Roland grabbed the towel and was headed for speeding in the room where, after opening the big closet, he chosen the first suit that had happened at hand. Complete satin blue with a white silk shirt is full of lace in the sleeves that around her neck.

"I think that this dear Count Mercier is not so clean as he appears. In any case it will not be easy to made forget him to Sophie. Love is blind, and what may seem so obvious to us the Baroness Lemaire can't even feel it."

Damien had followed him and was holding out a blue ribbon with which to bind their hair.

"Don't forget your art in winning the women. If you can not with your usual charm not fail to woo some other lady. Female jealousy works wonders! "

"I have no desire to come and then I'm really tired." Sophie was so sad to just want to go to bed as soon as possible. She had not billed the stubbornness of Camille who opposed his refusal.

"You must leave at least you will not have to think like you would shut up standing in this room!" She was about to respond when the maid came in with a light blue silk dress.
"This dress is not mine!"
"I know. I got some advice from Damien and we contacted the seamstress to make it real. " She began to touch her and her gaze had softened.
"Why did you do all this for me?"
"I want you to be happy and it is unnecessary that we repeat that Count Mercier can only give you pain and suffering. Why not start to look around?" We had not even thought for a moment before putting the superb tailoring establishment. Only when the mirror had returned her image, she was left open-mouthed. She had never owned a dress like that and even though she felt a little awkward, the preciousness of the tissue was unparalleled. The bodice was full of flakes in white satin and the skirt was embroidered with flowers in silver thread. The bustier was closed behind him with a tape clearly stood out on his olive skin. Camille had helped her hair styled in large curls on which she had placed some blue feathers. Before lifting boxes had opened and she had pulled out a pearl

necklace that her mother gave her before leaving the court. "You're wonderful! Each man will have eyes only for you!"

"Unfortunately, Charles was not present to be able to admire and maybe ask at least a compliment.

"Are you ready Mademoiselles?" Damien appeared at the door of the toilet and he made them a sign to follow him.

"Congratulations are both beautiful!" Sophie lodged with the neck to see if there was also behind the Count Chevalier. She had been astonished at her displeasure at discovering his absence, but she didn't want to ask your personal butler. She had not even questioned the fact that a boy of humble origins take part in all social events with his lord and to dress so elegant. She had come to regard his extravagance to a commendable permissiveness of M. Roland. Camille continued to spend much time in his company and, when she reprimanded for that behavior a bit shallow, she replied that one day she will discovere his secret. They had walked the route of the park that led to the grove of the Salle de Bal. The circular fountain gushing forming evocative play of soft light due to the countless torches just below each jet of water. The great vessels of gold held up turning them ready for the fireworks to end the show. At the center was placed a wooden platform and

a grand piano. A young musician had already started to make a heart-rending music. To his delight she had noticed the Count Chevalier sitting in the crowd who, however, seemed to be in good company. They were accommodated in the row just behind the two and when he turned she felt her heart to give her a somersault in chest. He was very handsome with his blue suit a satin so bright in contrast with the white shirt full of delicious ruffles. The lady next to him had blacks had hair so long that cover most of the shoulders. She wore a light pink dress and when she had turned she had discovered two languid eyes as blue as the sea. At the side of the mouth, she had a newly natural and not designed as they used to do most of the nobility. She didn't'say who she is and she left Sophie in anxiously waiting. She tried to fight with herself, repeating that M. Roland was just a friend and that se should be happy to see him with a young woman. Could mean that his teachings had borne fruit yet something made her shudder. She had always thought that what they had for Charles was true love but never had trembled so before his eyes. She understood that only the idea of a history with this woman would make her mad! Just finished the concert they had looked after him and she was flushed with anger when he took a path adjacent to the grove.

"Do you want pastries?" Camille was pulling the sleeve of the back to reality.

"Yes, thanks... And I wonder if the Count Chevalier needs (to) Damien, after all, he is his butler... "

"I don't believe that runs great risks. Ultimately it is in good company!" All this did nothing but complicate the situation. How could she explain his curiosity? Meanwhile Baron Dubois noted in the company of Madame du Barry, but without his wife. It had seemed a strange thing since the Baroness Coraline never missed an opportunity to participate in social events. Maybe she felt bad. In any case he had decided not to give weight to that absence. Had drunk a little white wine and she tasted a piece of chocolate cake when the Count Chevalier had approached with a firm step, friends. The girl beside her laughed taste and waving a fan in showy feathers.

"Good evening, Mademoiselle Lemaire! You are amazed with this dress of haute couture. Had made a generous bow to which he replied with a slight nod of the head. She could not hide his discomfort and did not want to look at the lady at his side. Roland before he had seen then he turned to Camille and had indicated that the mysterious girl.

"Mademoiselles, I introduce my sister Henriette. Damien, of course, already knows. " She wanted to sink into the ground. She had behaved like a fool and more like an unbearable jealous. Those three hours of uncertainty were still unable to open her eyes. That was the man she loved, and not the cold Count Mercier.

She was pretty breathtaking. She looked like a queen with that dress of your dreams. The idea to invite her sister, who was passing through Paris, to be able to make her jealous was found valid. At least he realized not to him indifferent. As soon as she had seen in the company of Henriette she was agitated and she had always followed him with her eyes. Now he was about to lead the game and win. He had never wanted to marry and he was a strong supporter of his personal liberty but Sophie had distorted his beliefs. Since their first meeting he had only think of her and he hoped for a future with her.

"Do you want to take a walk in the park? This evening breeze cools us from the heat of the day." She had not hesitated to agree.

"Henriette leave me with Mademoiselle Camille and Damien. We tuned in court!" They walked side by side with pleasant silence. They had stopped in the grove de l'Arc de Triomphe to sit on a marble bench.

"I would not be indiscreet to ask you a question so intimate, but I need to know your response". Sophie lowered his eyes and began to open and close her fan nervously.

"If I can do it I am very gladly to respond."

"What is for you, the Count Mercier? Please don't tell that he is a friend, because we both know that is not so." Did not want to be so crude but he could not wait any longer to know the truth.

"Maybe I was infatuated and I had exchanged affection for love. Your arrival at court helped me to open my eyes. I was a fool to lose all this time behind an illusion!" She seemed a dream to hear those words. He had no doubt of their veracity because now he knew that Sophie was unable to lie. And if he tried to do so would have exposed his eyes.

"I can then make love?" She smiled and looked at him straight in the eye.

"To be honest I don't wait more. Amaze me with your arts. But mind you that I don't intend to split up with any other!" He

didn't respond, but he only had to give her a chaste kiss on the forehead.

"Ever since I saw you the first time, I didn't think or admire any woman than you."

"I believe it for me will be difficult with your reputation as a libertine!" He could say sure of his feelings. Just call the biggest player on the scene. Sophie, if you really loved him, he would no longer hesitated to consent to his marriage proposal.

Excited about how she had carried the evening, she decided to head for their homes alone. Not because she wished to be accompanied by the Count Chevalier, but she felt that she had to first walk past the rooms of Charles. A person was pushing in that direction. She knew that was nonsense, but she had to do it. In the twilight the bedroom door was ajar and the door stood out a female figure from behind. She had tried to make plans to avoid being noticed. Charles had leaned forward to kiss her passionately. Her long blond hair disheveled had once thought that running to a lady but she would not jump to conclusions. When she turned, though the hall was dim, she had immediately recognized her. Madame Coraline Dubois herself. Embarrassed at being caught, before they had watched, then she ran away toward the stairs in a hurry.

"Mademoiselle Sophie, but you... what are you doing here?"

"Don't worry. Need not stutter, or that you give me an explanation. Now I understand why I've never made a proposal of marriage for all these years. I was a real stupid not to open my eyes before. That's for this reason that no wonder your cool this behavior." Shocked but not sorry for what it had happened, he looked at her almost with contempt.

"I never promised anything."

"Indeed. You have behaved like a true gentleman. In any case, don't worry about your story is not illegal hurts me more than it if not for the years wasted. Fortunately, tonight I discovered the man of my life and I wanted to announce it in person. I thought that you would have been happy for me. I regret that if I considered you like a friend' and not like a possible future wife, you should at least tell me your joys intimate. On the other hand I also understand that I was the right front for your reputation!" That outburst made her feel lighter and truly secure about what she wanted for her future. Without waiting for a useless and futile response she directed to her room to her well-deserved rest after a memorable day.

"Did you see that the ploy of bringing your sister to court has had its effect?" Damien was thrown on chaise longue next to the bed, while Roland had already undressed and settled into the cool silk sheets.

"You were really helpful in all respects. Tomorrow morning will be another surprise that will brighten your day." He had not finished the sentence that a footman was present in the room.

"Sorry but monsieur Mercier wants to see you with some urgency." The friend had given him an amused glance.

"The news fly!" Roland had fallen out of bed and he ordered to do sit in the lounge. He had no desire to get dressed so he grabbed his robe in silk burgundy and he bound the hair and then he gone into the adjoining room. Monsieur Mercier was walking up and down before the great journey in marble.

"What good wind brings you in my room at three am?" The man was in obvious embarrassment. His usual cool composure had given way to an expression almost bewildered.

"Sophie... or Mademoiselle Lemaire has just discovered me in the company of a young woman..."

"Oh God, better than in the company of a man!"

"Don't make jokes in bad taste. The lady in question is married and I don't want that a scandal was born... "

"And what am I supposed to do?" The count had laid his hands on the back of the chair.

"Please convince her not to talk! I felt that perhaps one of you there is more than just friendship and... " Roland felt compelled to clarify his feelings, which Charles, out of cowardice, he never did.

"I love her and I think that she discovered to prove something for me."

"Exactly, so nobody better than you can persuade her not to mention the incident."

"Don't worry you have my word even if I believe that it is not necessary. Sophie has only just discovered the pleasures of love and I don't think that she has some time to think about anything else... Even if you have very hurt."

"I know, and I regret but I could not give her anything more than just friendship." Roland had called a valet to accompany him to the door. Only when the count was already back, he had felt the need to tell him one last thing.

"Let me express my opinion. I don't want to offend you, but I never thought that a man as serious as you could share a bed with a woman of dubious origins and with a past as a prostitute as Madame Dubois!" Charles didn't objecte, but he always wondered how he done to discover and hide it to Sophie. He could only recognize that the gentleman was really him because, although he had useful information in hand to open the eyes to the girl, he left that time had run its course.

She slept little and she thought much. She had come to the conclusion that her love for Roland had blossomed much earlier than she had believed. Perhaps the evening of his arrival to Versailles during the dance in the hall of mirrors. She got up and after a copious breakfast she had donned a cream-colored dress. She was finishing her long hair coiffed auburn when Camille had come like a fury in his room.
"Hello dear! But how beautiful you are in the early morning!" The friend looked triumphant and eternal happiness.
"So I think that it's time for you that I reveal the coveted secret of Damien... and, for some time now, even yours!" She gave her a steaming cup of tea and pastries. Before she taste one she

directed at the window overlooking the park bathed in sunlight. "You're right. After all, after last night, now you know the Chevalier family complete!" Sophie looked at her with open mouth.

"I don't understand what you mean."

"Damien is the brother of Roland. His mother had conceived with a man in Austria. At his death he met the count with who she has remarried." She had burst into a guffaw, as she had not done for months.

"I must say that they had chosen a nice ploy to get him to the court."

"It's all what I wanted to tell you!" She took her hand and she had to look into her eyes.

"Oh so I'm afraid."

"No. You must be happy because I'm in seventh heaven. We decided to get married this winter and going to live in the north. Or better to return to my beloved land." She embraced her with enthusiasm and started to cry.

"What good news! Your joy is mine!" Camille had come off and took her hands.

"So joining me soon right?"

"What do you mean?"

"I don't think that you can say no to the next proposal of marriage of Roland. And then we can continue to live together and more in our beloved Picardy" She was ashamed to admit that it was also her dream to return to her country. As loved Versailles and Paris, she lacked the immense expanses of flowers in summer and snow in winter. Completely absorbed in her thoughts to try to understand how important it was Roland she had not noticed that both lived in the same region of France. Seemed a twist of fate. As if the count was her guardian angel instructed to bring her home.

"I have asked to marry him. But now I am sure if he will consider me the happiest woman in this world." A maid knocked on the door.

"Sorry, Mademoiselle Sophie, but the count Chevalier is waiting in his apartment with a guest. He had been asking questions, but he rushed hastily towards the corridor. Camille smiled because she was already aware of what she saw and she knew that this Monday, June 12, 1769 would be remembered for a lifetime.

When he was seen that she was entering, he hold your breath. Her auburn hair seemed more bright as ever and her eyes were calm and relaxed.

"Hello, did you call me monsieur?"

He alluded to the two attendants of room to leave them alone and then he knelt before her.

"You are beautiful! I will continue to tell you every day of my life if I may!" A extravagant mode to ask her for marriage.

"I don't want is to hear this for all my future! If this is a proposal of marriage I am happy to accept it." He was getting up and he was kissing her, but she stopped him.

"First let me make you a fitting note. I don't want divedi with any woman. I want this to be clear."

"Ever since I saw you I didn't have eyes for you and I have neither courted nor responded to the overtures of other noblewomen. You have my word. Before I knew I didn't know what love was now I could ruin everything for a sordid history outside of marriage. Believe me!" She given her hand to help to get up and she left him to kiss her with passion. With care he had taken from his jacket a little box with a ring with diamonds forming a flower.

"But it's wonderful!"

"Never as you." He had put him on his finger and then he brought her into the living room.

"Come I show you a person who has done a little street to see you again." When the footman had opened the door, he had to support her. At the sight of her father, she thrown around his neck.

"But what you do here? And why did not you noticed?" Then she looked at Roland quizzically.

"My dear came at the invitation of the count. I asked permission to make you his proposal and I agreed that it was in hopes that you too want". The man's eyes were shining, but could not hold back her tears. He was tall and very thin. His large dark eyes and olive carnation stress their familiarity. Roland was involved in aid of Baron Paul, in evident embarrassment.

"I known your father for some time because we have economic interests together. When I spoke to you I had yet to meet but I must say that his description reflects reality. It was not that of a blind father for the love of her daughter but totally true!" She thrown himself on the big chair near the fireplace and she started to cry.

"Oh now my heart burst with joy. Because Mom is not with you?" The father came up to her and he sat beside her.

"She wanted to follow the restoration of our new castle at Amiens. Our property was adjacent to the count. Think you continue to live near us." It was not easy to imagine a future so happy. The expected an amazing castle, a wonderful husband and very kind, parents are always present and dear sister-like friend Camille. So it was worth leaving the magnificent palace of Versailles as soon as possible.

The characters of this novel are a figment of my imagination, while the figures of Louis XV and Madame Du Barry are real but freely interpreted.

I wait for your opinion on my blog:

www.samilla.wordpress.com

Louis XV (1710-1774)

Madame Du Barry (1746-1793)

Versailles Chateaux, in un dipinto di Schloss, 1722

www.ingramcontent.com/pod-product-compliance
Ingram Content Group UK Ltd.
Pitfield, Milton Keynes, MK11 3LW, UK
UKHW020235250726
13967UKWH00001B/373